A Duck, Duck, Porcupine! Book

My Kite Is Stuck!
And Other Stories

Salina Yoon

SCHOLASTIC INC.

For Cameron and Bergen, with love!

ISBN 978-1-338-54110-6

12 11 10 9 8 7 6 5   20 21 22 23 24

Printed in the U.S.A.   40

First Scholastic printing, January 2019

Art created digitally using Adobe Photoshop
Typeset in Cronos Pro
Book design by Salina Yoon and Colleen Andrews

Three Short Stories

One

My Kite
Is Stuck!

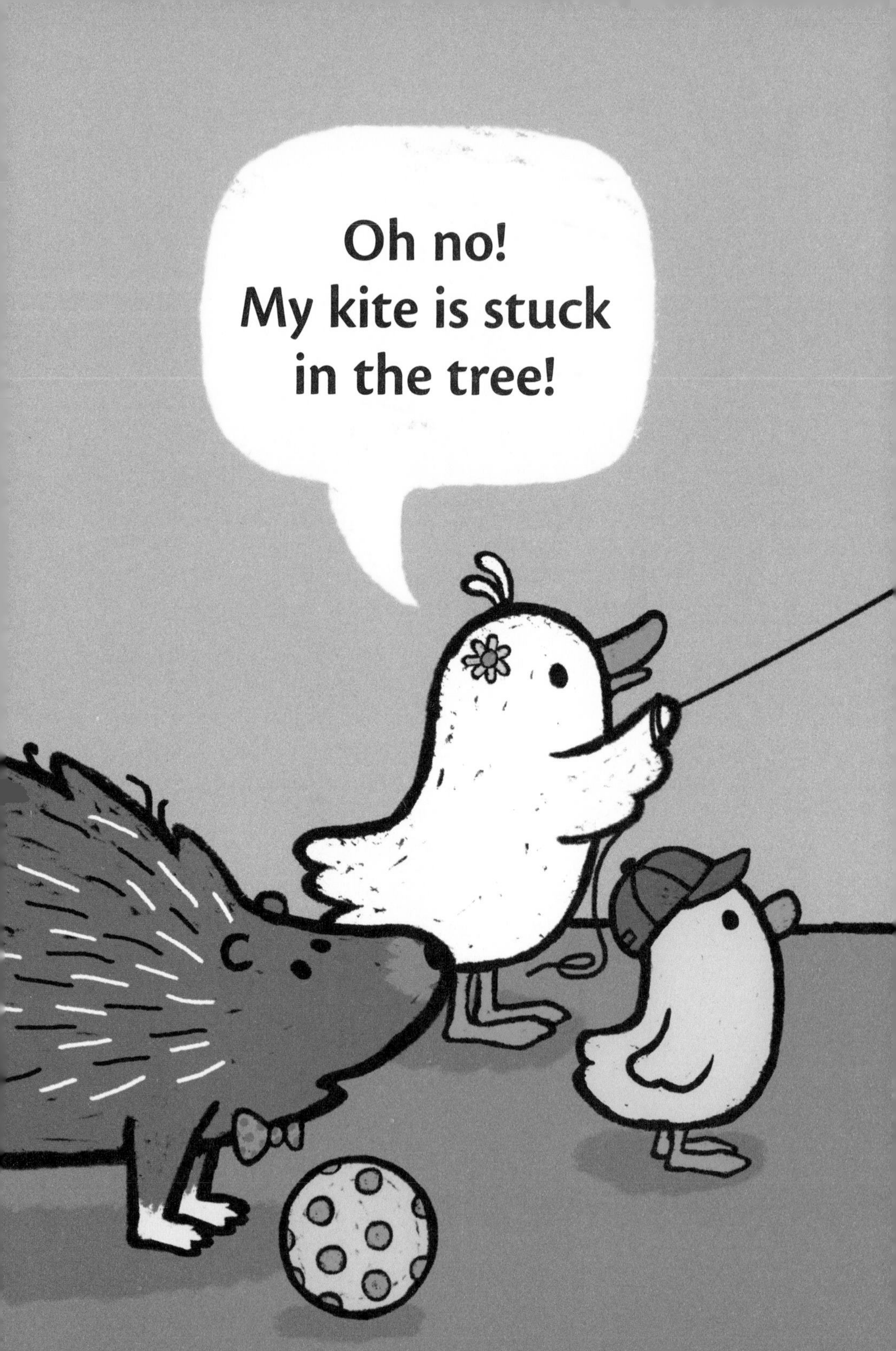
Oh no!
My kite is stuck
in the tree!

I can't fly up that high yet.
Don't worry, Big Duck. I will knock it down with my ball.
Kick!

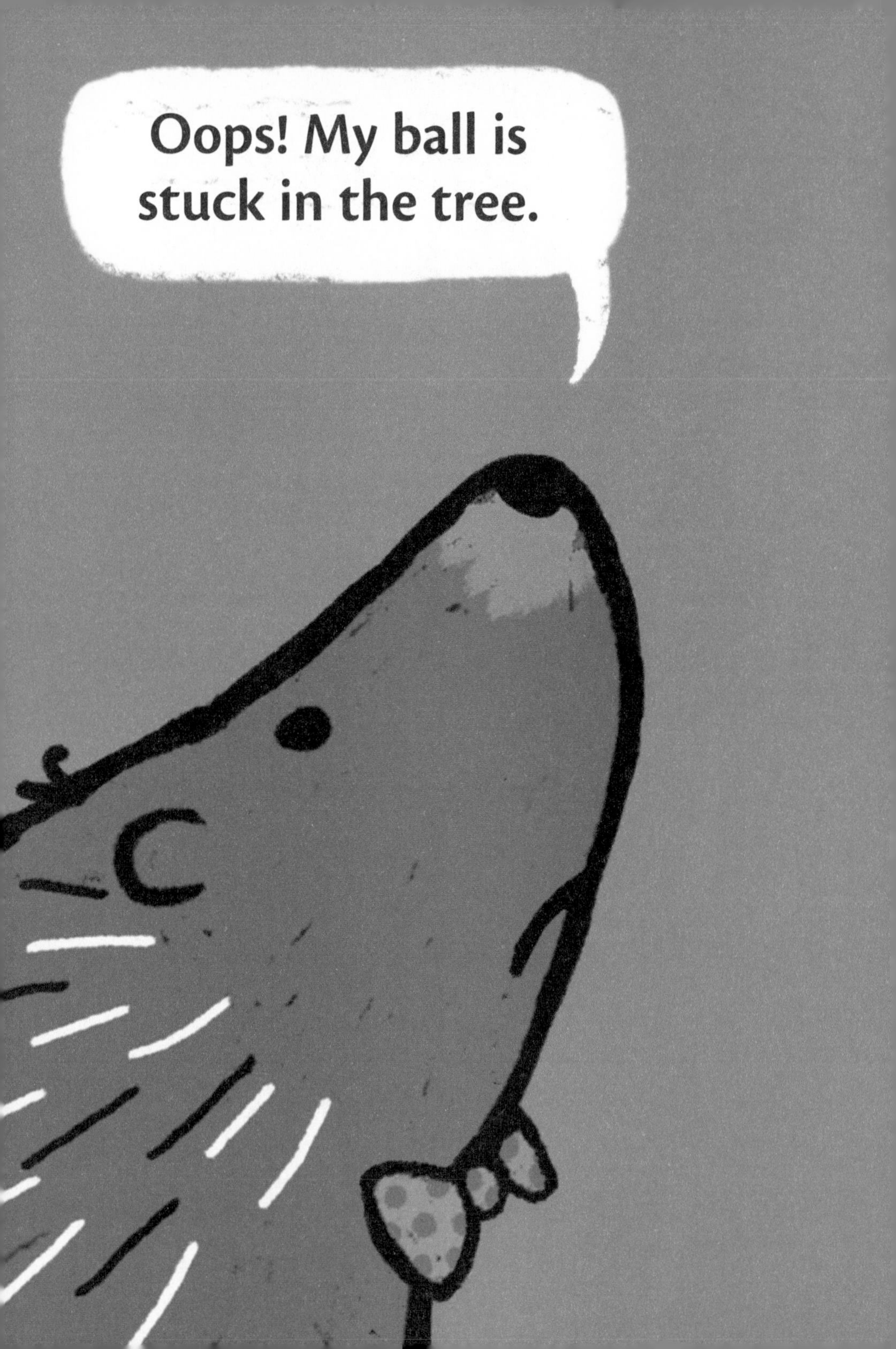
Oops! My ball is stuck in the tree.

Don't worry, Porcupine. I will get it down with Little Duck's hula hoop.

I don't think your kite, my ball, or Little Duck's hula hoop is coming down from the tree.

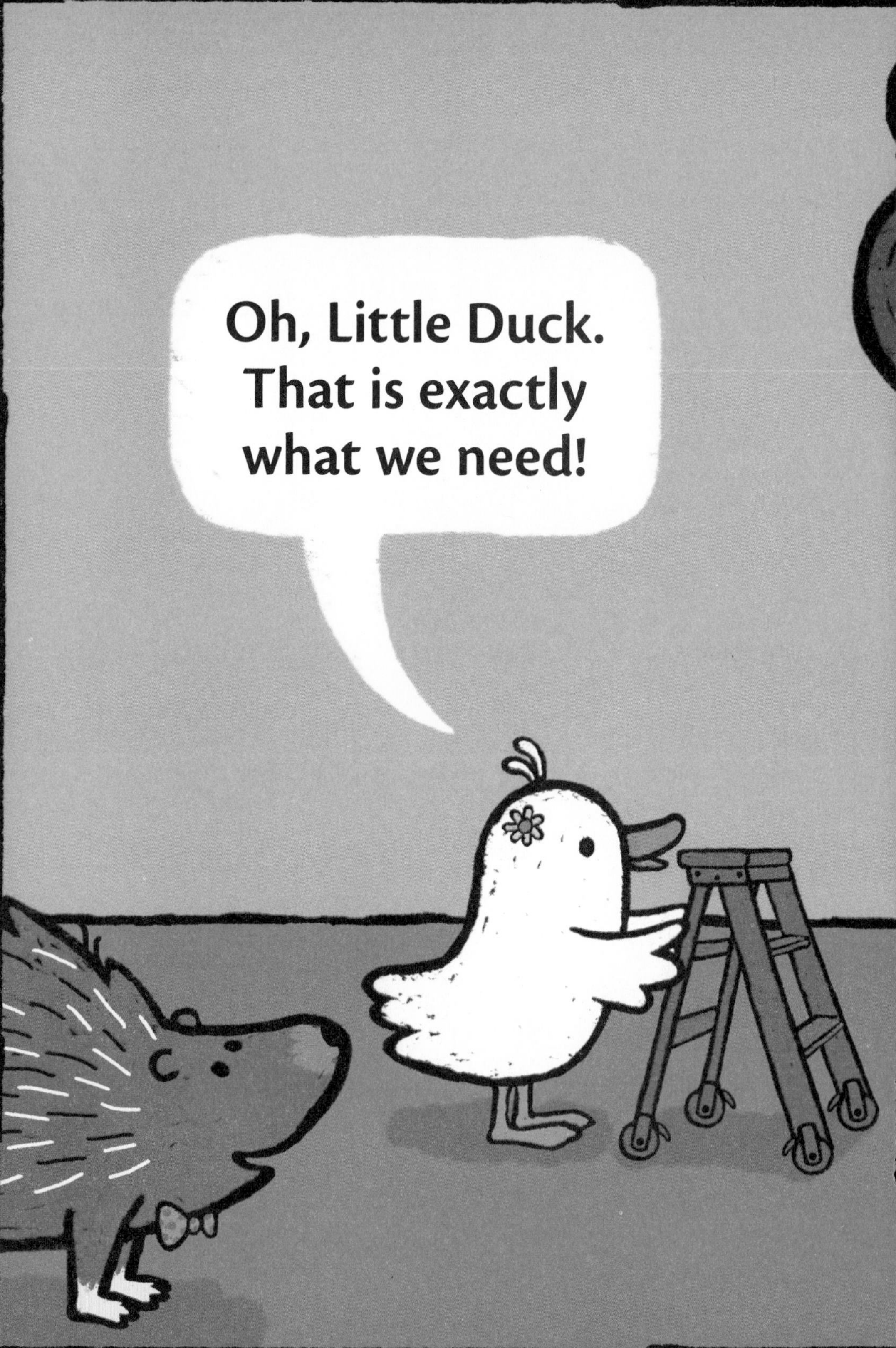
Oh, Little Duck. That is exactly what we need!

There is just one thing left to do, Porcupine.
What's that, Big Duck?

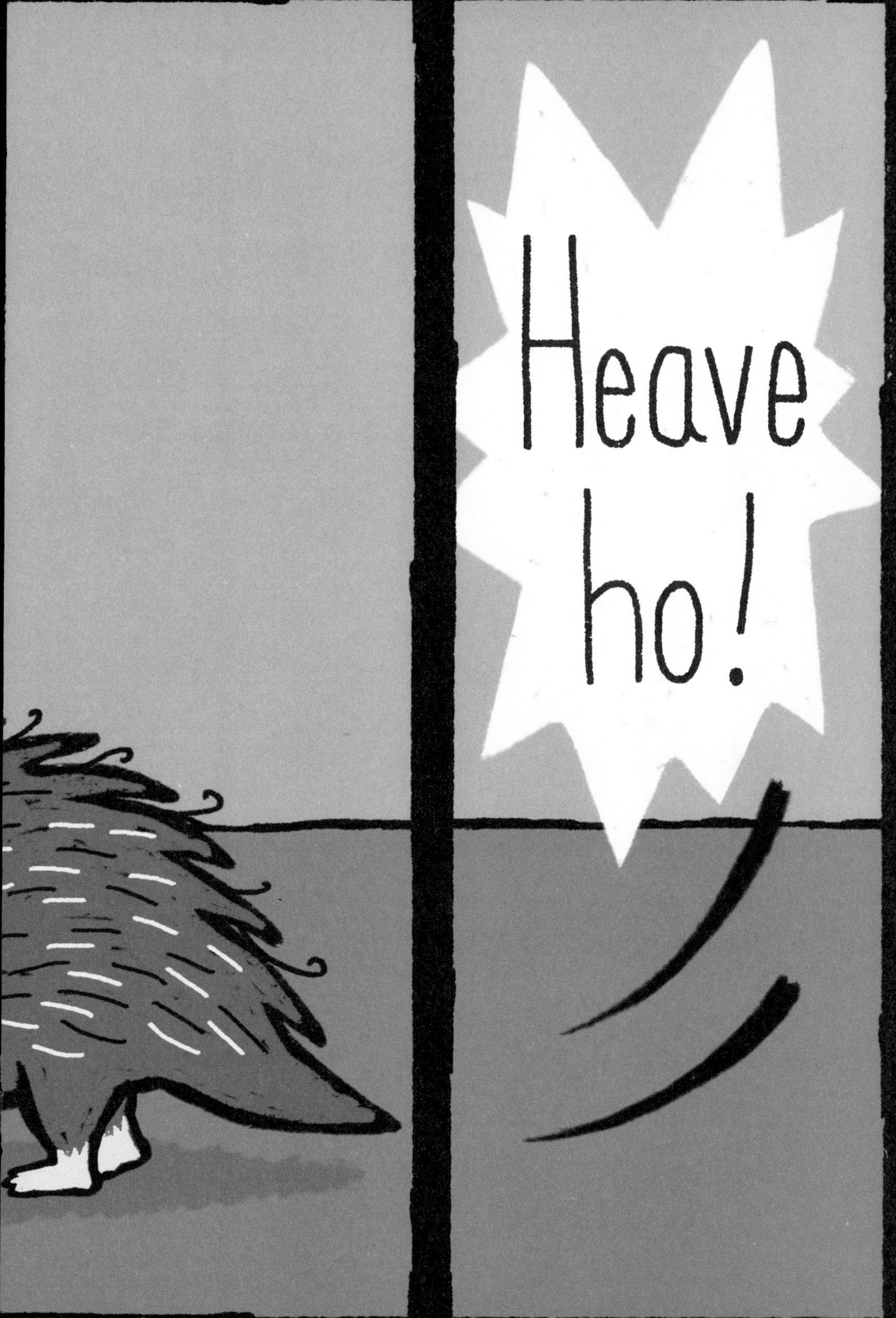
Heave ho!

Two

A New Friend

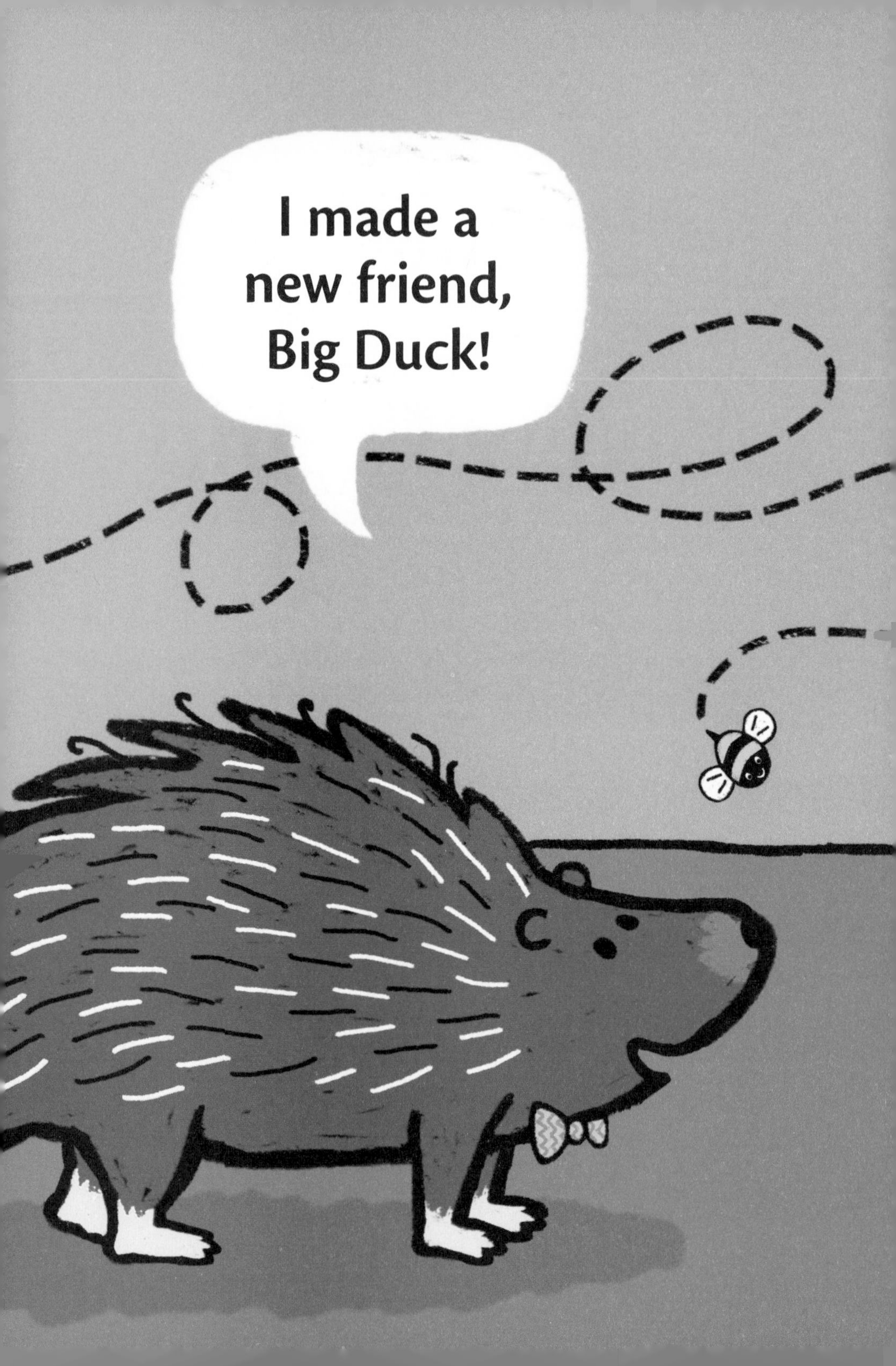
I made a new friend, Big Duck!

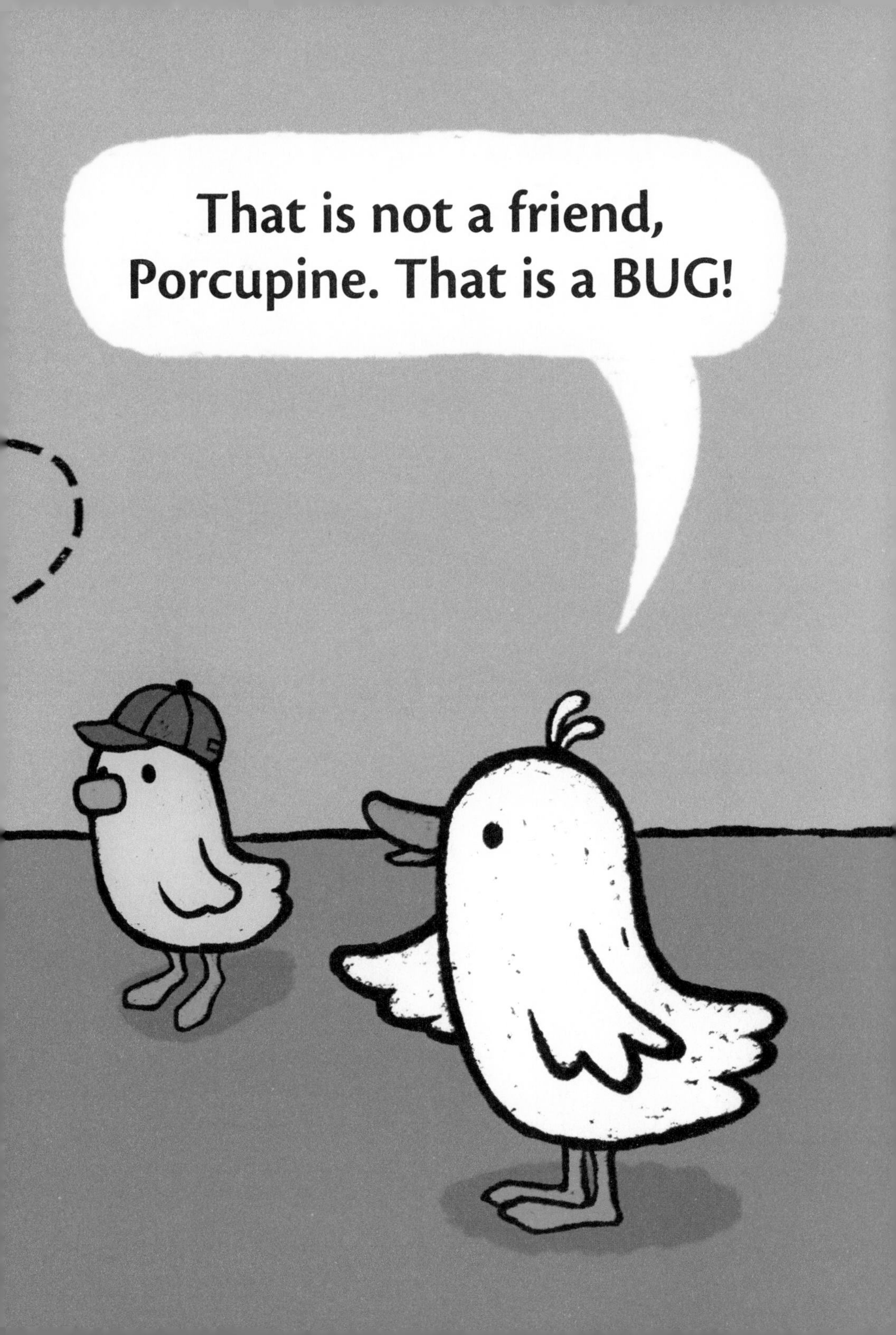
That is not a friend, Porcupine. That is a BUG!

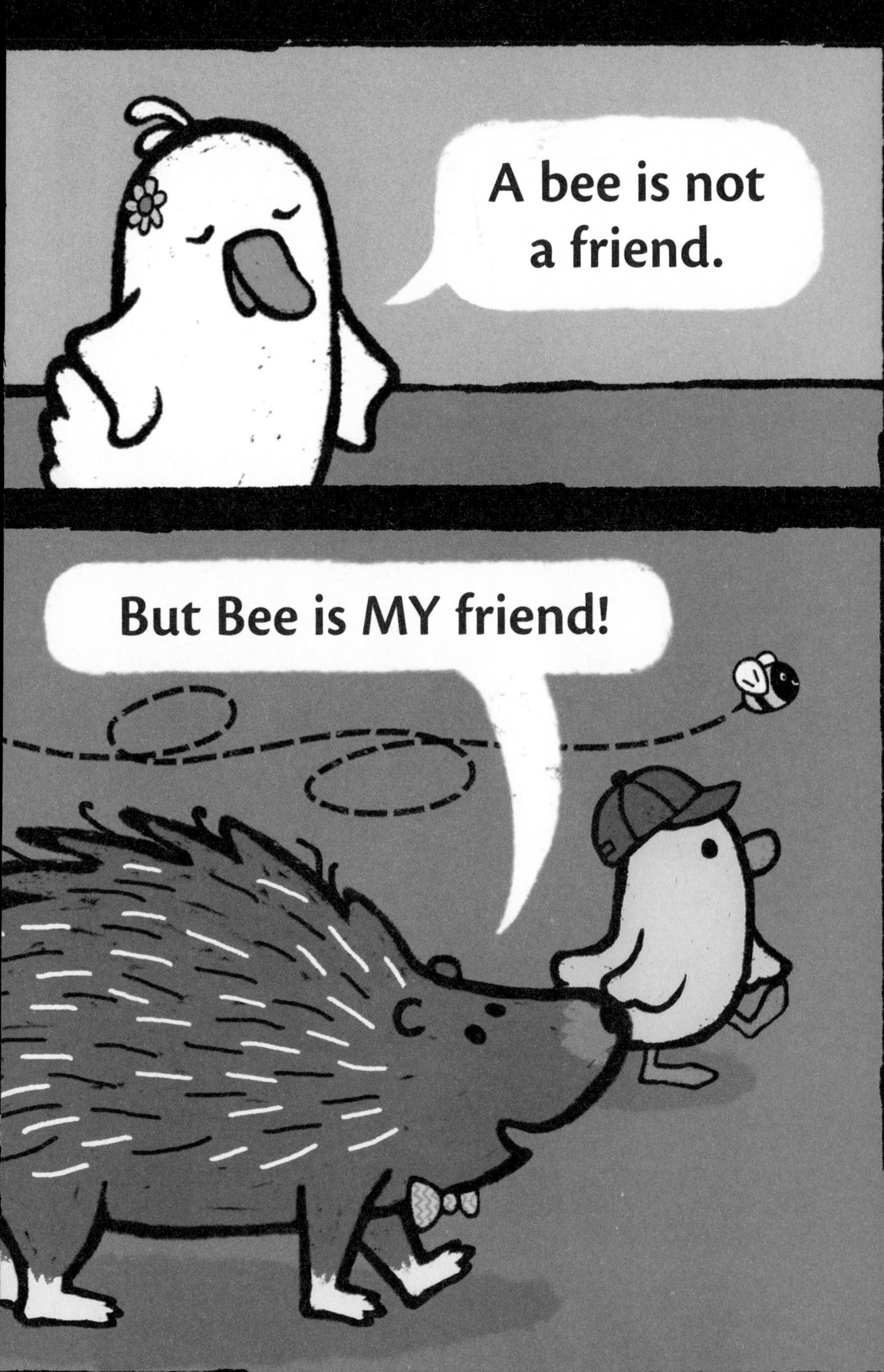
A bee is not a friend.
But Bee is MY friend!

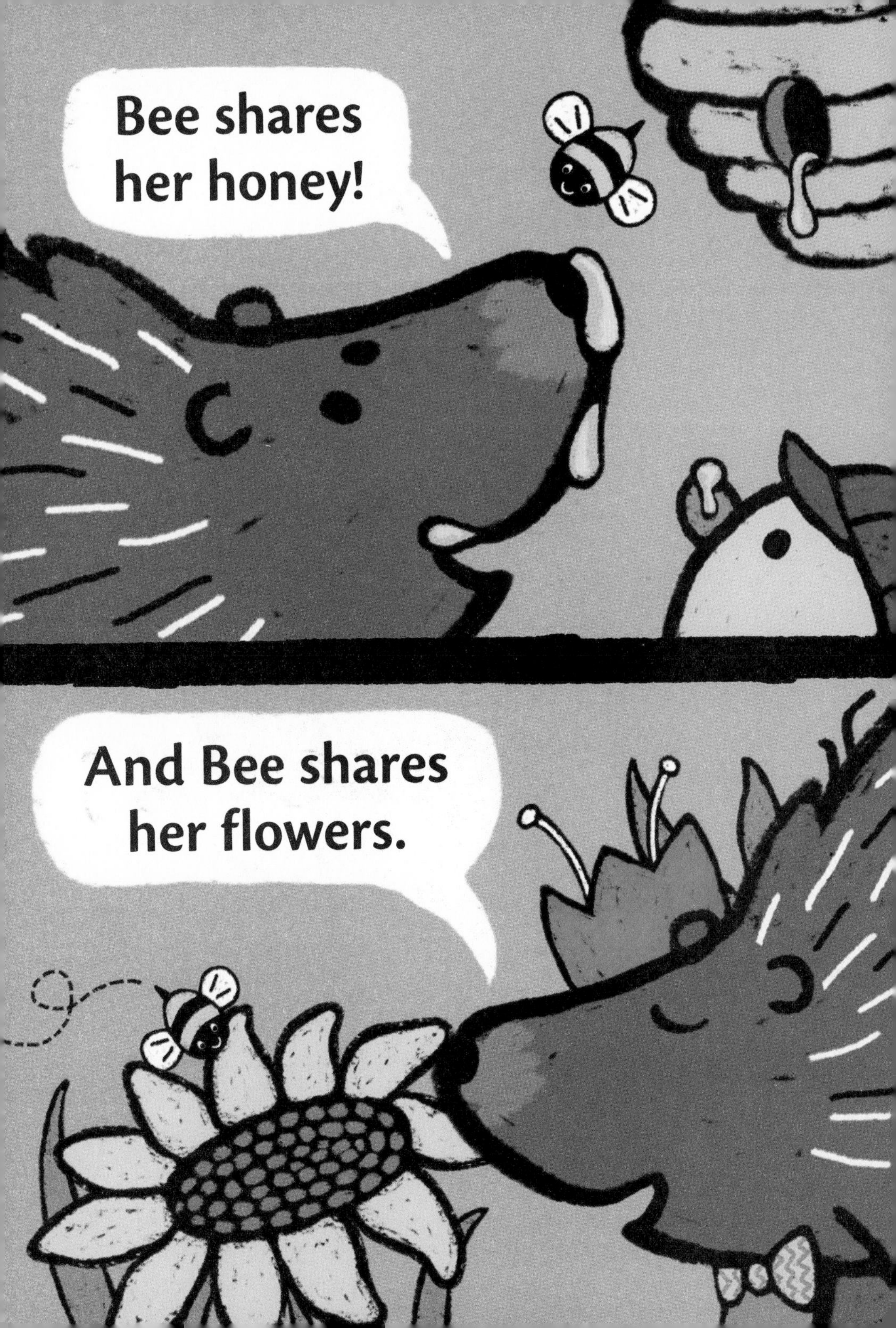
Bee shares her honey!
And Bee shares her flowers.

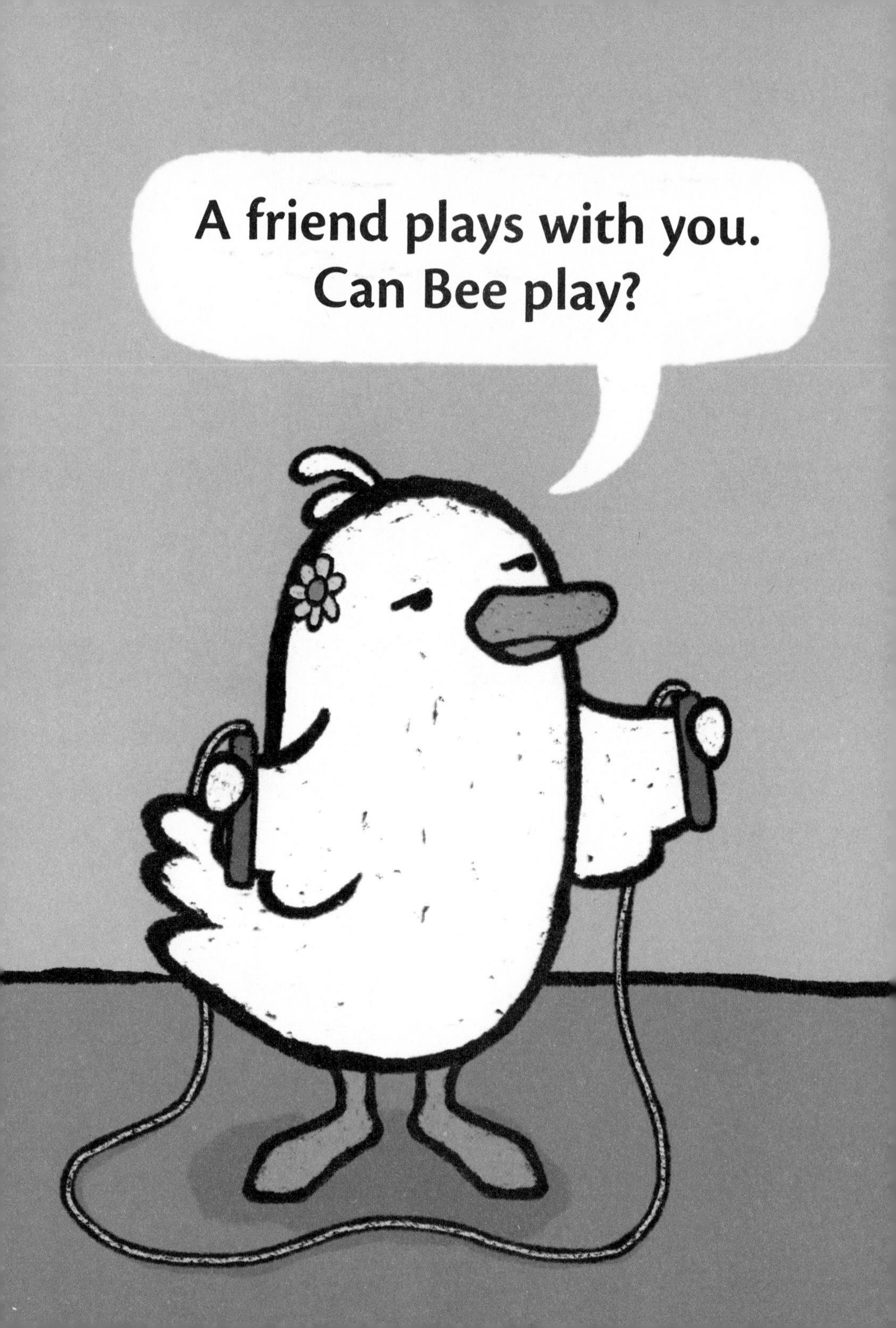
A friend plays with you. Can Bee play?

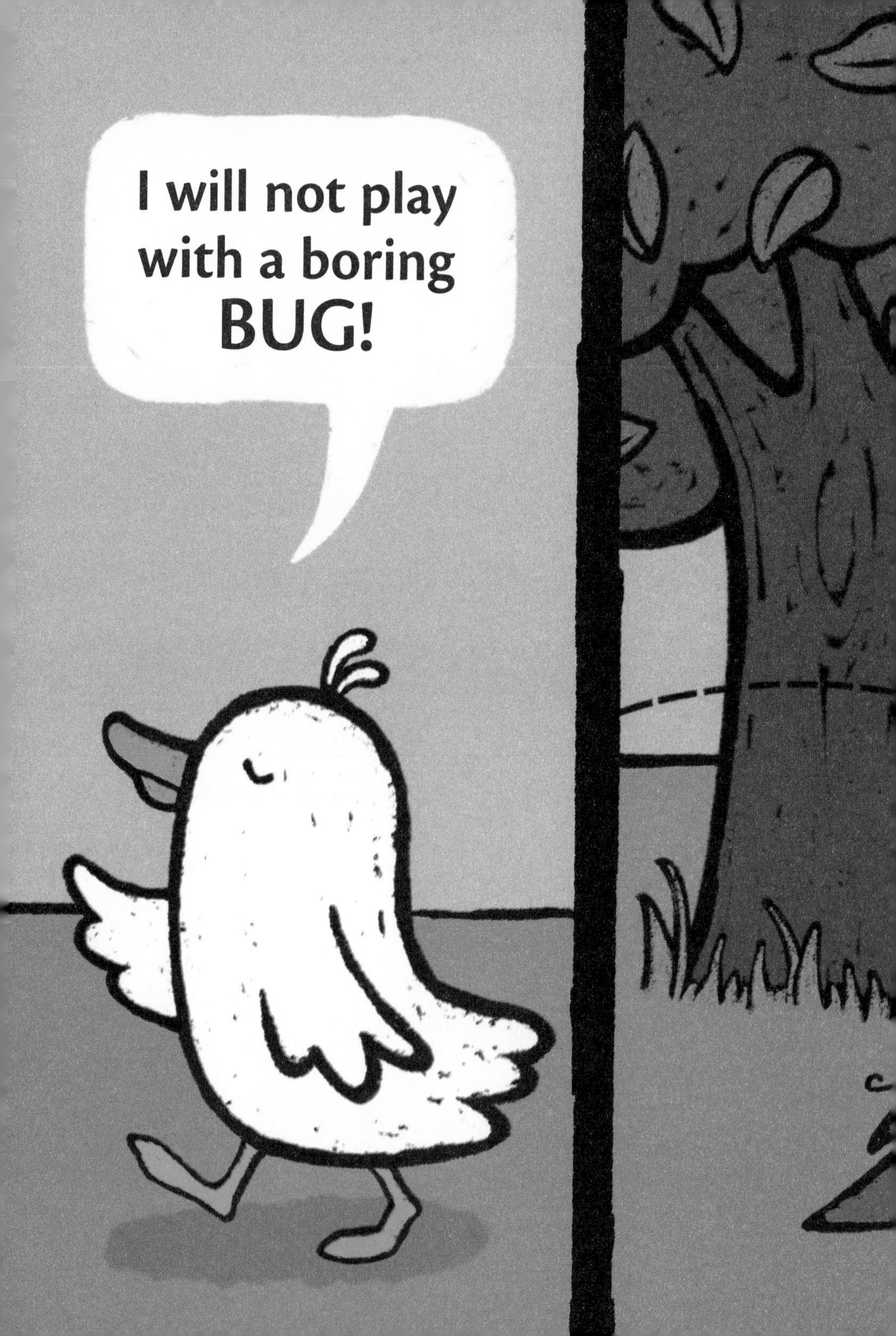
I will not play with a boring BUG!

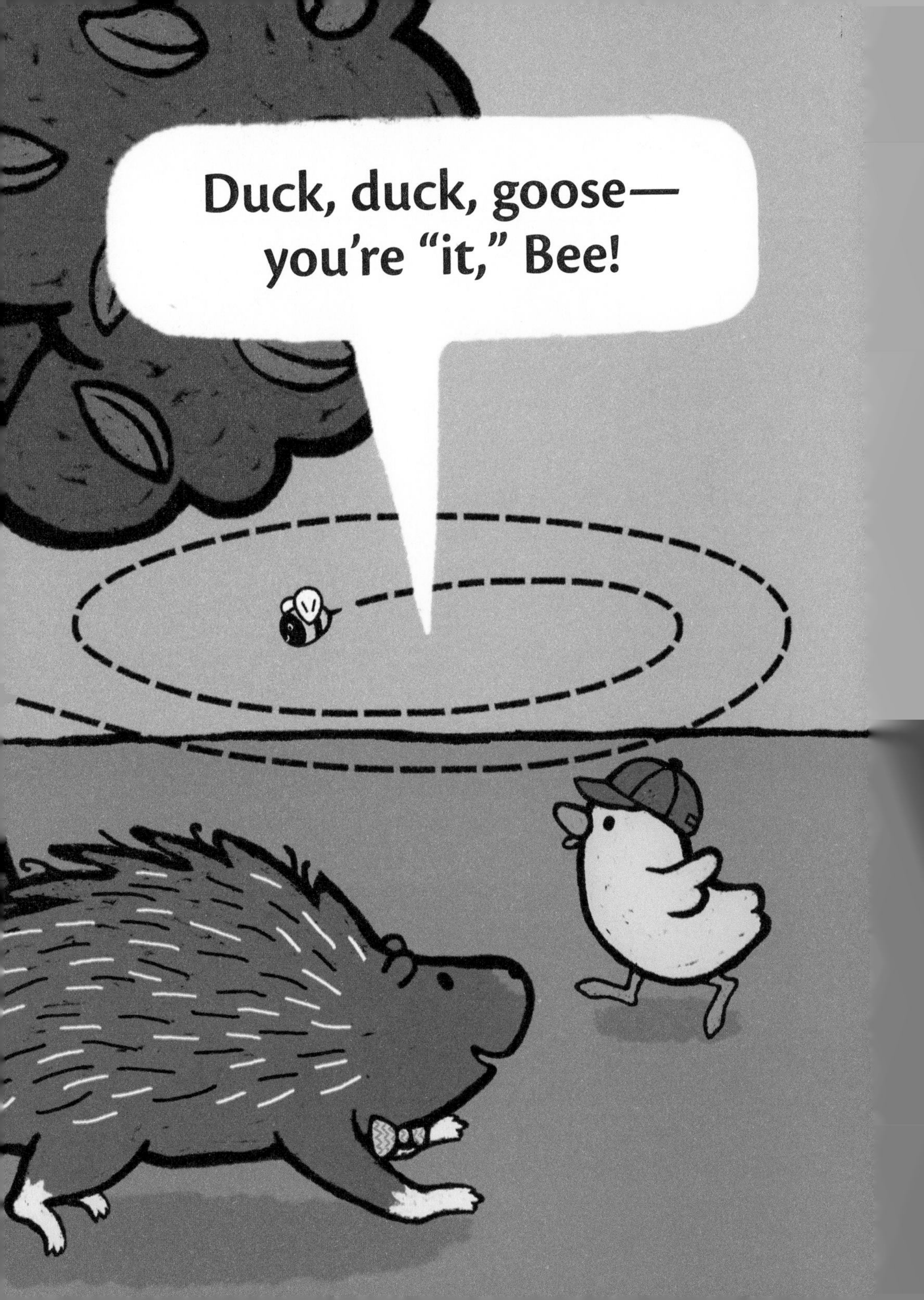
Duck, duck, goose—
you're "it," Bee!

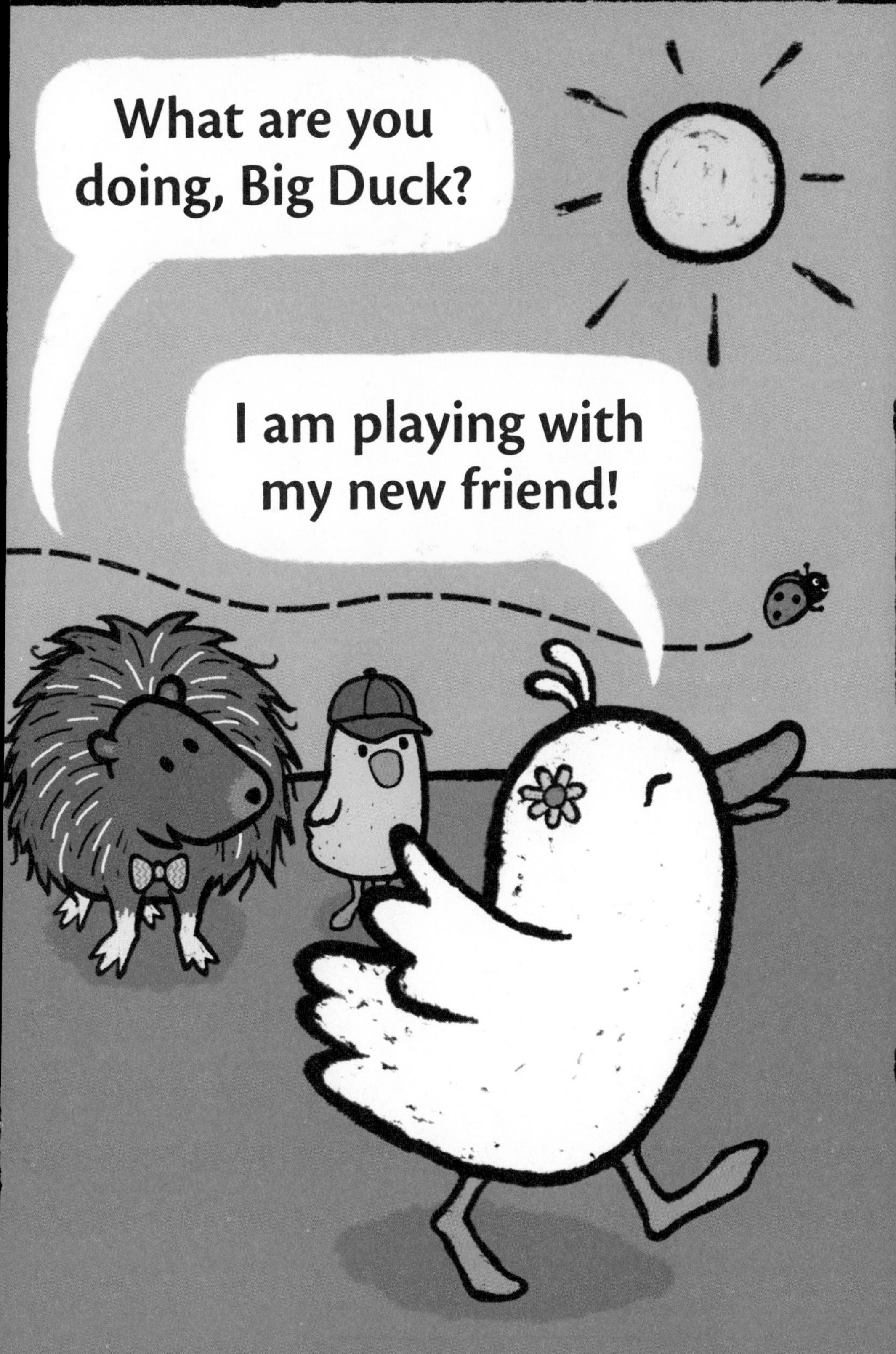
What are you doing, Big Duck?
I am playing with my new friend!

But that is a bug!

Yes it is—a LADYbug! Bugs are fun.

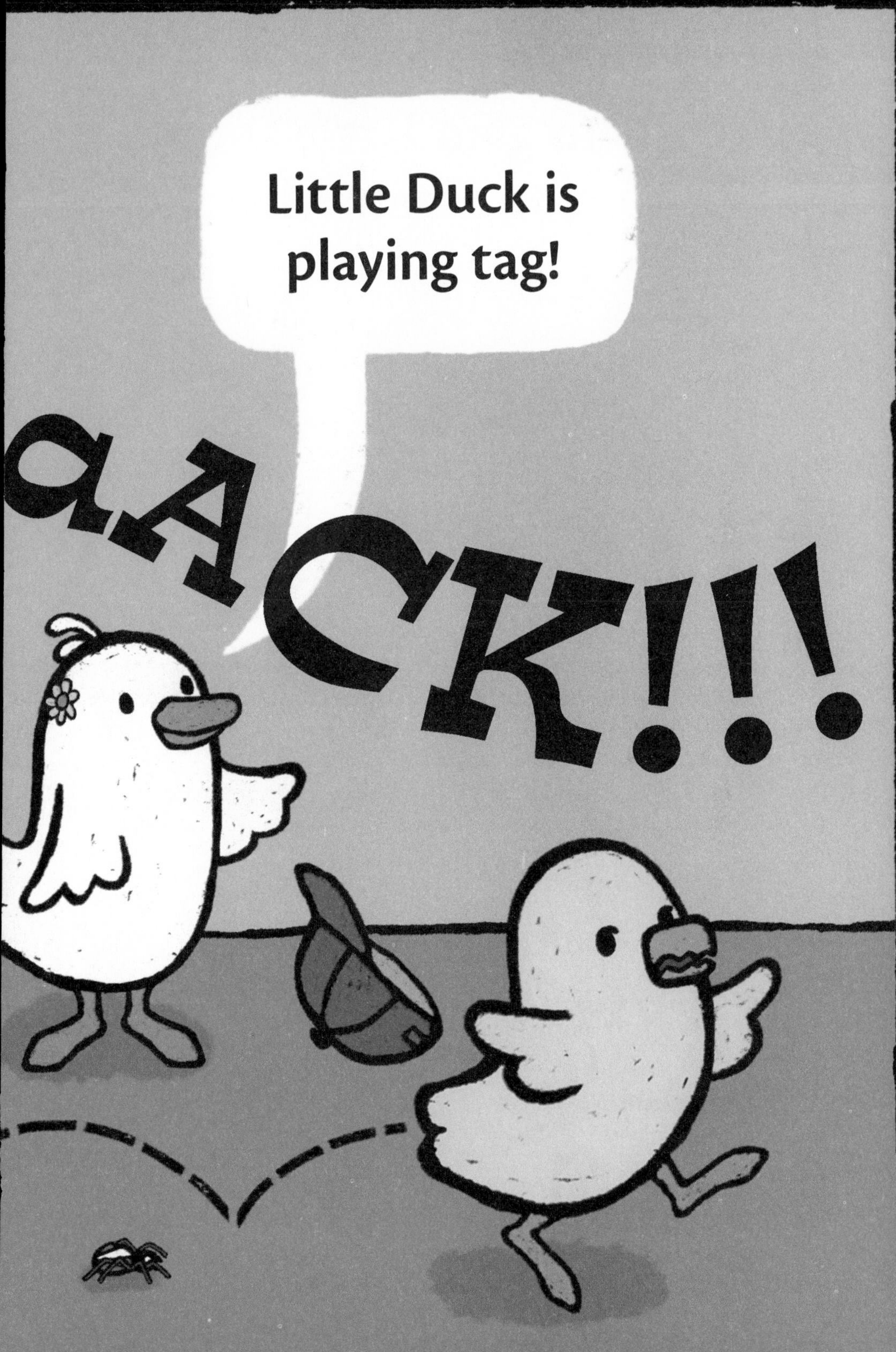
Little Duck is playing tag!
aACK!!!

Three

Best Lemonade Stand

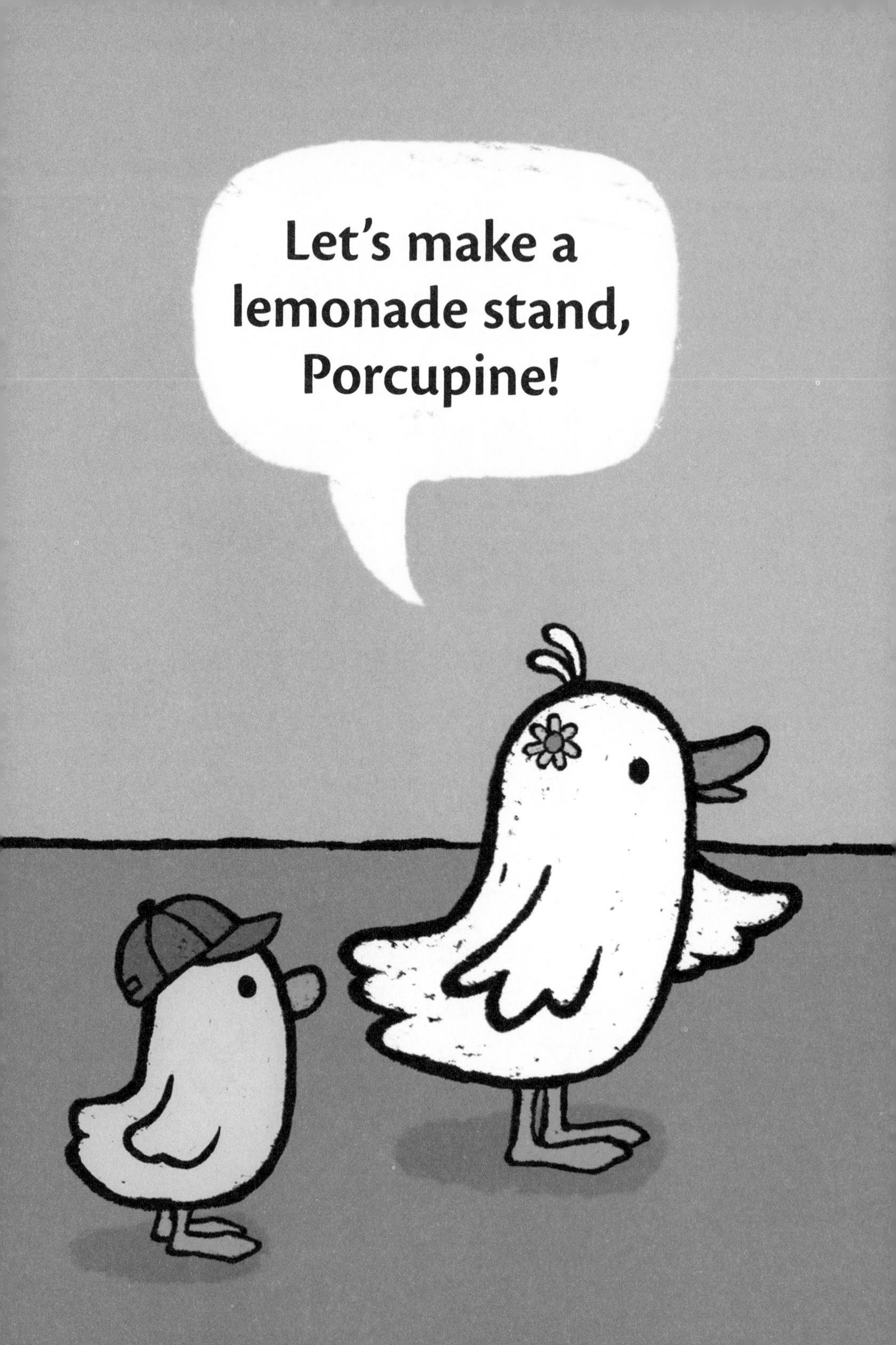
Let's make a lemonade stand, Porcupine!

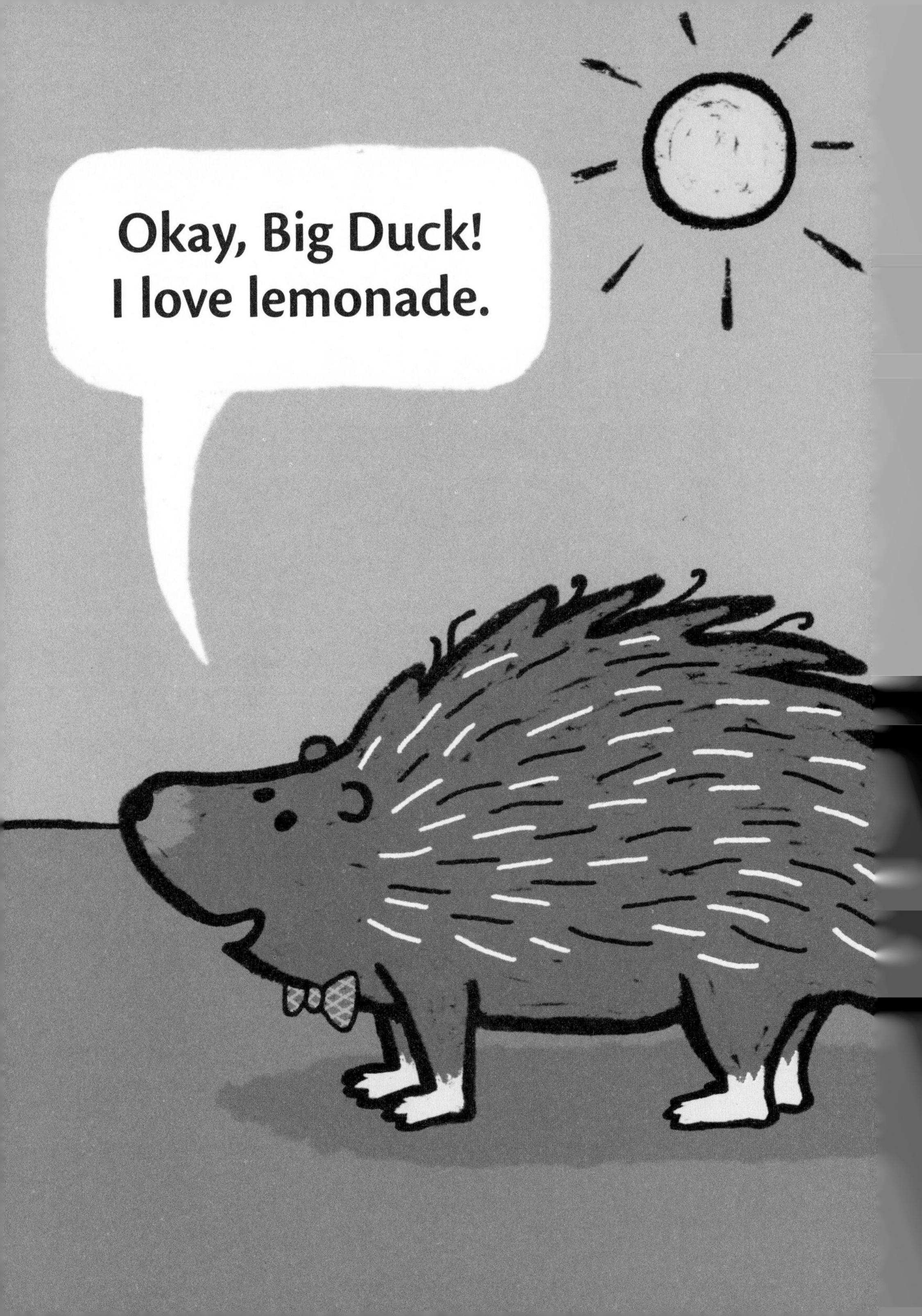
Okay, Big Duck! I love lemonade.

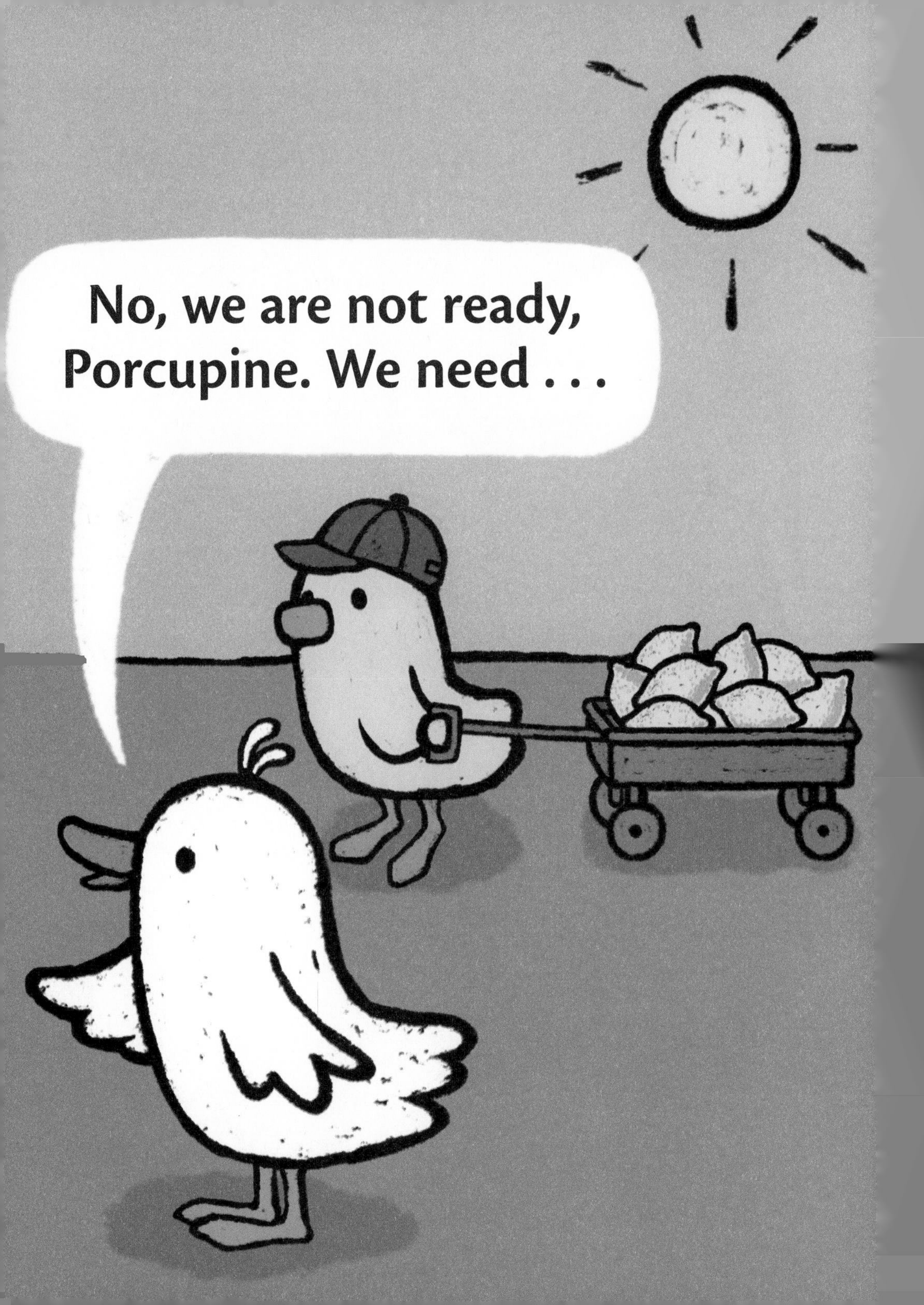
No, we are not ready, Porcupine. We need . . .

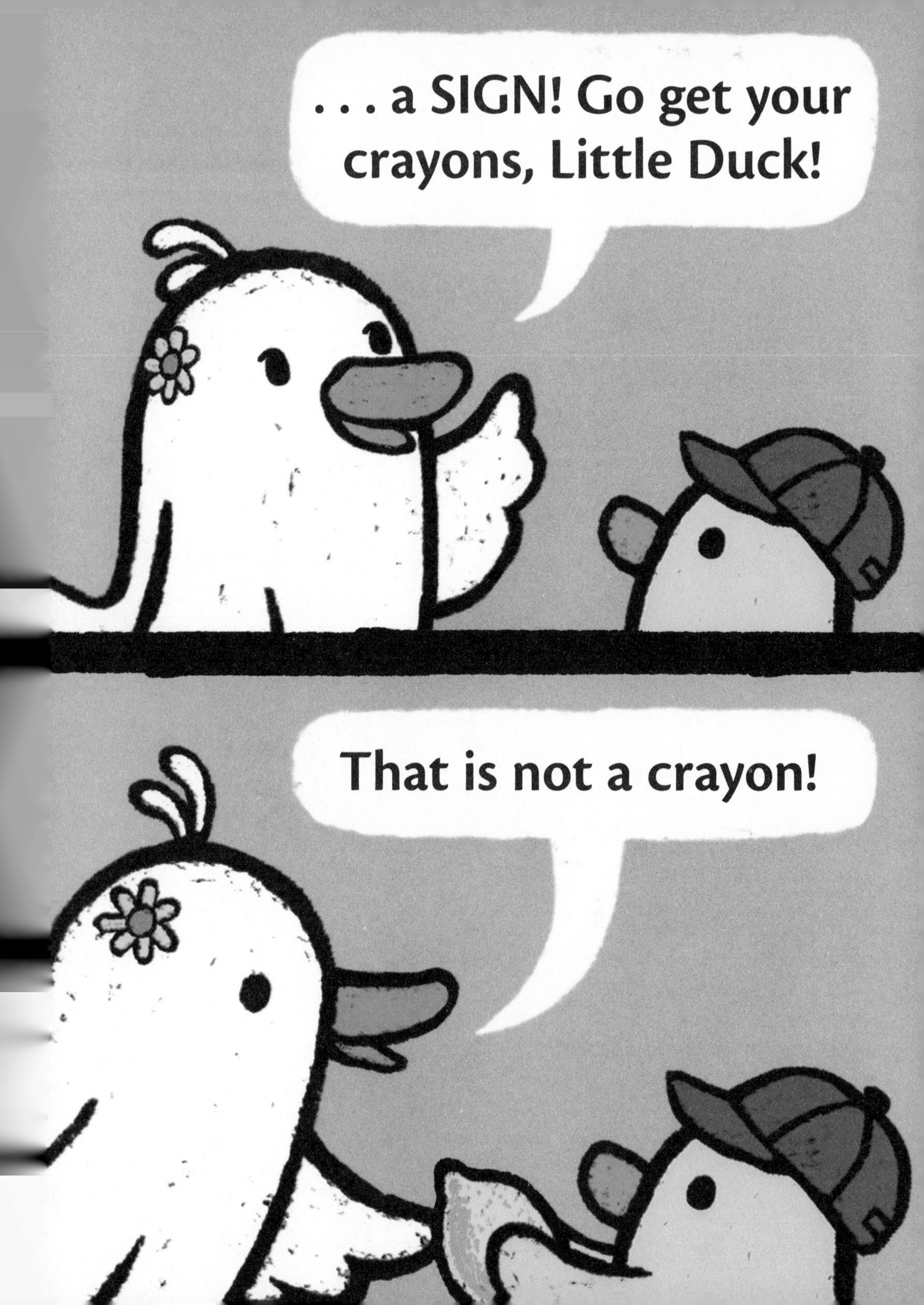
. . . a SIGN! Go get your crayons, Little Duck!
That is not a crayon!

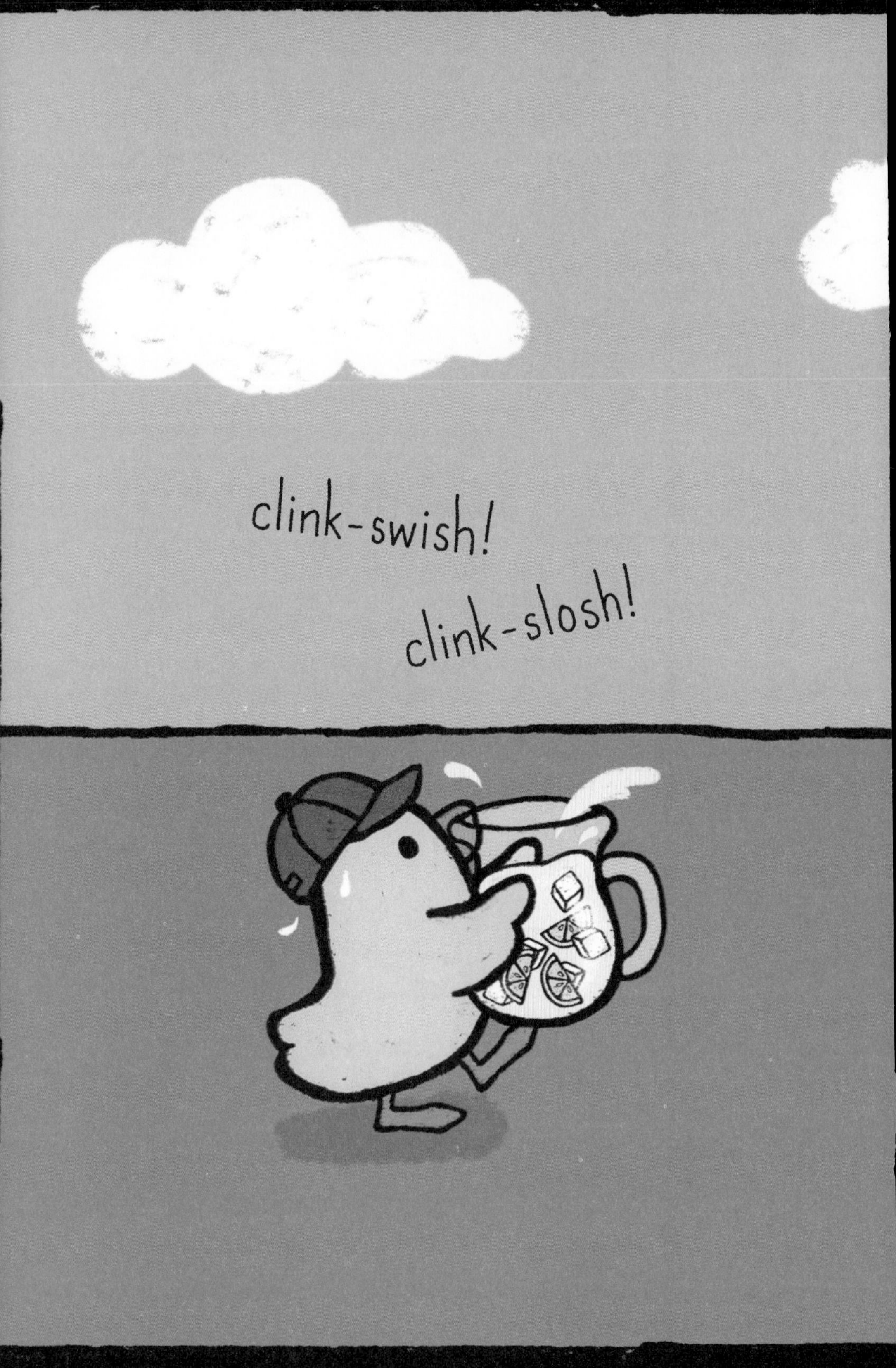
clink-swish!
clink-slosh!

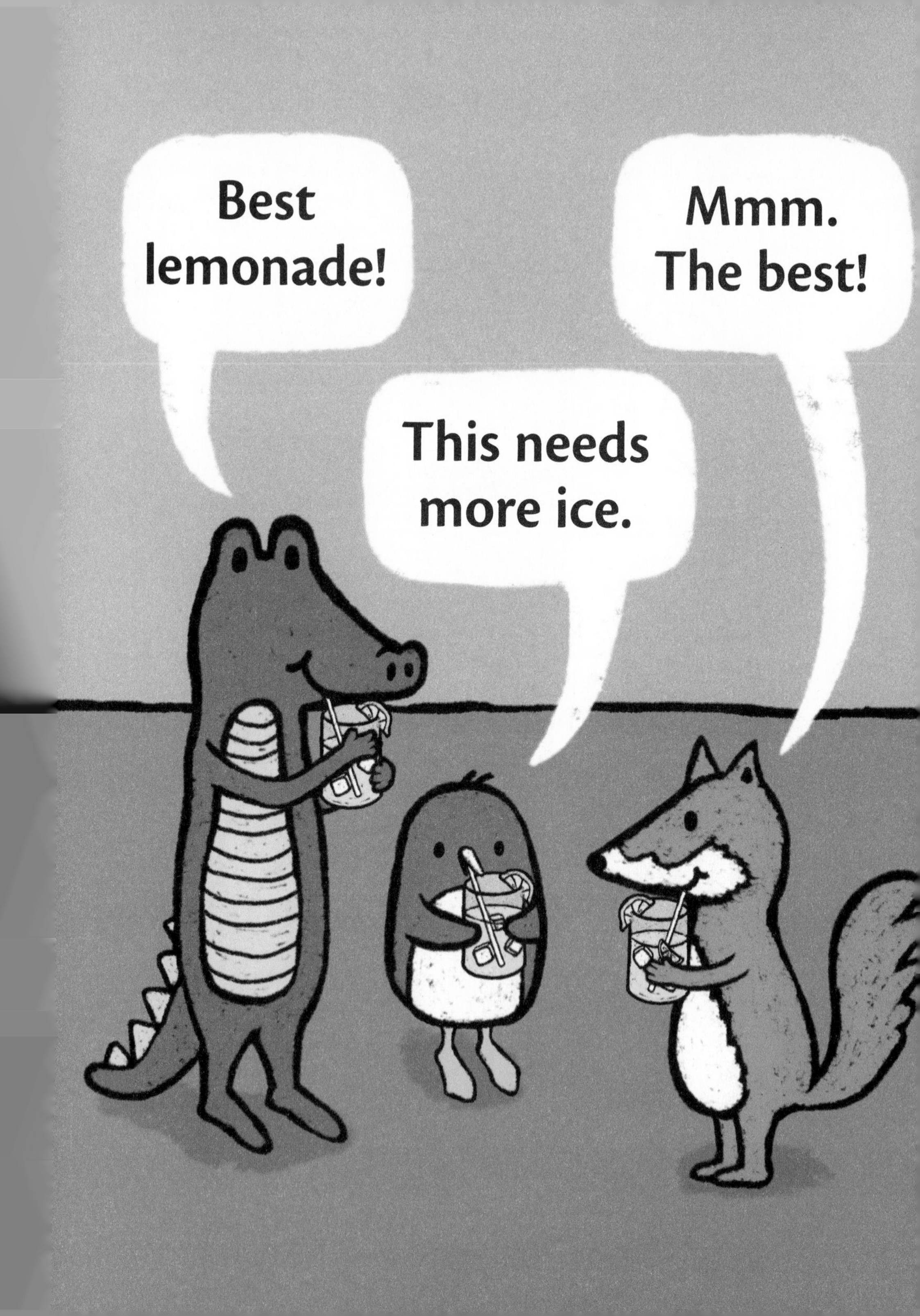
Best lemonade!
This needs more ice.
Mmm. The best!

Curtains make all the difference!
Lemonade
Fresh Squeezed
25¢
a cup
sip!
sip!